Illustrations by Ivan Earl Aguilar

Printed in the United States of America.

ISBN: 978-1-4907-4677-7 (sc)
       978-1-4907-4676-0 (e)

Trafford rev. 10/01/2015

Trafford
PUBLISHING®

North America & international
toll-free: 1 888 232 4444 (USA & Canada)
fax: 812 355 4082

RECOMMENDED by US Review of Books
(Professional Reviews for the People)

"This series of books is designed to open up some difficult dialogues with children in a safe and trusting environment …"

"With a big soccer match against the Moosehead Lodge approaching and the potential for danger in the deep dark wood, the reindeer are in for a coming-of-age event that will leave them changed forever…"

"This book can prove to be a useful tool to instill important values in young children…"

AWARDS EARNED
RUNNER-UP

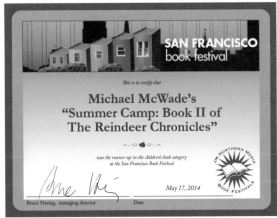

HONORABLE MENTION

Dedication

To Mom (1932–2010), I miss you.

I know you would be proud of my reindeer stories. Now and for those yet to come.

You sure did love frogs.

Foreword

When Mike first told me about The Reindeer Chronicles, I wasn't surprised. I knew that, eventually, the creative writer in him was bound to emerge with his goal being to entertain as well as to introduce some of life's lessons to youthful audiences; he has re-created characters that most children are familiar with and can relate to (Santa's reindeer).

By giving the reindeer who pull Santa's sleigh distinctive looks and personalities (see back cover), he will use these characters in an effort to show children respect for themselves as well as others.

Mike has always had a distinctive relationship with children, whether it be coaching youth sports or raising his niece (she recently earned a Master's degree). His goal is to reintroduce his audience to some old-fashioned ideals that seem to have been obscured in our fast-paced social-media society—truthfulness, personal integrity and open-mindedness are just a few.

Mary Kay Scully
Friend and Editor-in-Chief

SUMMER CAMP

BOOK II OF THE REINDEER CHRONICLES

WRITTEN BY MICHAEL MCWADE

ILLUSTRATED BY IVAN EARL AGUILAR

"**B**e quiet or we'll get caught," said Donner to Dancer as they approached the edge of the building. They had just arrived at summer camp that afternoon, and it was now almost dark outside. They were crouched against the building known as the barracks, which is where the reindeer slept. The girls slept in a separate barracks, and the two were divided by a gravel road, which the two mischievous reindeer could now see only by the light of the moon.

As they began to quietly cross the road, they were nearly knocked down by someone running toward them. "Watch out!" said the intruder as he crashed into them.

"Shhhh" said Dancer, and he could see that it was another boy reindeer that had stumbled upon them.

"I'm Scooter," he said. "What are you guys doing?"

"We're going to scare the girls by putting this frog in their barracks," said Donner, and he lifted up the cage he was holding, with a frog inside. "You can come with us, but you have to be quiet."

"**C**ool," said Scooter. He took a closer look at the frog in the cage. It was dark green with copper-colored patches all over its skin. It looked like the frog had a little gold crown on its head. *That's odd*, thought Scooter. Then he asked, "How did you get the frog to agree to this?"

"We promised to show it where the giant lily pads are in Misty Lake." And the frog just smiled and said, "*Rid-dip.*"

The three of them then quickly crossed the moonlit road and approached the door to the girls' barracks. They opened the door very slowly, slid the frog out of the cage, and ran back to the side of their building. "Do your stuff, little froggie," said Donner.

The frog stood up on its hind legs, put its hands on its hips, adjusted the crown slightly, and said in a low female voice, "My name is Dottie." Then it disappeared through the door. It didn't take long before they heard the girls begin to scream.

"What's that noise?"

"It's a monster!"

"Get it out of here!"

The boys could not stop laughing as they hurried to get back to their beds.

"Rise and shine!" yelled Captain Jack as he blew his whistle.

Blitzen slowly opened his eyes and began to wake up, as did the rest of the boys. He saw Captain Jack standing in the doorway, eyes wide, wearing a dark green cap. Captain Jack was in charge of the boys during summer camp.

"Breakfast in five minutes," he said and turned and walked out of the barracks. There was a collective groan as the boys slowly made their way outside and to the dining room.

Vixen entered the cafeteria and sat down at one of the long tables. She hadn't slept very well last night. Mostly because she wasn't in her own bed but also because there was quite a lot of commotion as some sort of creature had gotten into the girls' barracks.

The other girls—Comet, Cupid, and Dasher—were instructed by Mrs. White to sit next to her. Mrs. White was in charge of the girls at summer camp. She was the oldest reindeer Vixen had ever seen, with gray fur, a wrinkled face, and glasses. She wore an odd-looking white hat that tilted to one side.

Vixen looked around the dining room. There was a kitchen area where several deer she didn't know were scurrying to get breakfast ready—an assortment of leaves, fruits, and nuts.

The room was made of wooden logs stacked on top of each other. There were three other tables. At one of them sat Blitzen, Dancer, Donner, Prancer, and another boy she didn't recognize. She smiled and waved at her best friend, Blitzen, and he waved back.

Vixen took a good look at how her friends had changed in the short time since the field test. Donner was bigger and stronger than the rest of the boys, and had tied his red flag around his neck like a handkerchief. *He is such a jock*, she thought to herself. She had seen Blitzen often during the summer, but the tuft of fur on his chest looked like it was thicker, and his tail had turned all white. Dancer was still sleek and slender, and had white patches of fur on his side and a small one above his nose. Prancer was still smaller than the other boys. His fur was a pinkish brown, and he has the most beautiful violet eyes.

Her girlfriends had changed as well. Dasher looked bigger, and the white streak on her side looked more pronounced. Cupid was staring off into space as usual and had a shiny, new silver chain hanging around her neck. *I'll have to ask her where she got it*, thought Vixen. Comet was the most unique-looking of her girlfriends. Her fur was a darker brown than the rest, and she had dark ears and small black patches all over her fur. She always wore an ankle bracelet made out of black leather, with pink fur and silver buttons on it. She said she got it from her grandma. *What a funky deer she must have been*, thought Vixen.

As for herself, Vixen loved to wear lots of different bows in her hair. Since it was summer, she thought she would wear something colorful, so she picked out a yellow bow with red polka dots on it.

"ATTENTION!" yelled Captain Jack. He was standing at one end of the room with Mrs. White next to him, who had a very angry look on her face. "I've been informed," he began to say as he turned and looked at the very unhappy Mrs. White, "that a frog was in the girls' barracks last night,  causing quite a stir. And if I find out someone put it there on purpose, there will be severe consequences."

Donner and Dancer gave each other a quick nervous glance and went back to eating breakfast.

After breakfast, the girls went off to dance class and the boys to soccer practice.

"Now listen up, my young bucks," said Captain Jack, addressing the soccer team. "This summer, we will once again be playing our rivals— the team from Moosehead Lodge. We have never beaten them."

"We will this year, sir," said Donner, but the other reindeer looked around hesitantly.

"Yes we will, my boy. And do you know how? Speed, that's how. Moose may be big and strong, but they are slow. We are going to be the fastest team on the field and run circles around them!"

Captain Jack blew his whistle, and they ran out to the field for practice.

Dasher really didn't like dance class. She could hear Mrs. White giving instructions, but she wasn't really paying attention.

Why should I be standing here, twirling around in one place, when I can be running free on the soccer field? she thought as she looked longingly across the camp to where the boys were practicing. To feel the wind in her hair and the sun on her face as she raced across a bright, green field was what she really wanted.

"Pay attention or Mrs. White will scold you," Vixen told her.

"I don't like dancing," Dasher replied.

"How could you not like dancing? It's so much fun!" said Vixen as she twirled around Dasher, smiling.

Prancer really didn't like soccer practice. He didn't understand it, and Captain Jack was always yelling at him to stop eating the grass or staring off to the sky.

What's the point of kicking a stupid ball around a field when I could be dancing? he thought. Dancing was fun! He had asked Mrs. White to let him into the dance class, but she said no—it was only for the girl reindeer.

He heard a whistle blow, and someone was calling his name. He looked down, and there was the ball at his feet.

"Kick the ball!" everyone was yelling. "Kick the ball!"

He just looked down at the ball and sighed.

"Don't worry about it, my friend," said Donner as he came up and kicked the ball away. Donner was always looking out for Prancer, and he was very grateful.

He looked up; he saw Blitzen and Dancer on the other side of the field, talking to another reindeer.

"**S**o it WAS you who put the frog in the girls' barracks," said Blitzen. "I knew it."

"Yes, it was me, Donner, and Scooter," said Dancer, and he introduced Scooter to Blitzen. "It was hilarious."

"Better hope Captain Jack or Mrs. White doesn't find out, or you'll be in real trouble," Blitzen warned.

"Well, I'm not going to tell them," said Scooter as the other boys agreed.

"Say, what were you doing out all by yourself that late at night?" Dancer asked Scooter.

"Um, I was exploring the woods," replied Scooter a little hesitantly.

Dancer and Blitzen looked at each other, puzzled, but they didn't say anything else as some sort of commotion was happening in the middle of the field. They ran to check it out.

When they approached, they saw Dasher standing in the middle of a group of boys.

"I don't see why not," she was saying with a very mad look on her face.

"What's going on?" they all said at once.

"Dasher wants to play on the soccer team," they heard someone say. By this time, a big crowd had gathered.

Suddenly, Captain Jack appeared, towering over the crowd. "What can I do for you, young lady?" he asked Dasher.

"My name is Dasher, and I want to be on the team," she said boldly. "I bet I'm faster than any of these boys."

Not me, thought Donner, but he didn't want to embarrass his friend. Besides, he knew she *was* fast from racing her last summer.

"Oh really?" said Captain Jack.

Somebody in the back of the crowd yelled, "Girls don't play on boys' teams!"

"**W**ho made up that stupid rule?" said Dasher as she was beginning to lose her patience.

"Now calm down, everyone," said Captain Jack. "Didn't I tell you earlier, boys, that we need to beat Moosehead Lodge with speed?"

Donner and Blitzen looked at each other and nodded knowingly, and then Blitzen said, "Why don't we have a race?"

Dasher looked at them with a big smile on her face.

"Sounds like a fine idea," said Captain Jack.

Some of the boys grumbled, but most of them agreed—not that they were going to argue with Captain Jack, anyway. He instructed them to line up at one end of the field.

"When I blow my whistle, you will all race to the midfield stripe. If Dasher beats more than half of you, we let her on the team."

"Don't worry," said Donner to Dasher.

"You can do it," Blitzen told her.

Prancer just looked at all of them and thought he'd rather be dancing than running.

Dasher let her mind go blank. She had to concentrate. The whistle blew, and off they went.

*R*un, run like the wind. *Run like you never have before*, she thought.

And she did. When she got to the finish line, she was second only to Donner in the race. Immediately, Donner, Blitzen, and Prancer ran up and gave her a big hug.

"Congratulations, Dasher. You are now a member of the soccer team!" said Captain Jack.

Dasher was so happy. She turned around and saw that all the girls had gathered to watch the race. She ran to the middle of them, and they exchanged high fives and cheers.

That evening, Dasher and Prancer were alone before dinner. Prancer said to her, "I'm so happy for you, but I envy you. I'd rather be in dance class than playing soccer, but I don't have the nerve to try out for it like you did."

Dasher gave him a hug and said, "You will, someday."

That night, the young reindeer were huddled around a campfire. As they were exchanging stories and cooking up some dinner, Cupid began to daydream, thinking back to what happened on a cold night last winter.

*   *   *

Cupid's parents were cleaning up before they went to bed. Her mom was in the kitchen; her dad was in the living room. They gave each other a quick nervous glance across the room because they knew if it was going to happen, it was going to happen tonight.

Cupid couldn't stop staring at her new shiny necklace. Her birthday party was fun. All her friends were there including Vixen, Dasher, and Comet. They had played lots of games and, of course, eaten cake. Reindeer really love cake. The necklace had a bright, shiny silver chain, and at the end of it was a little chubby angel shooting a bow and arrow. It was really pretty.

Cupid looked out the window of her room and saw a lot of stars glowing in the sky. One in particular seemed to be brighter than the others. As she stared at it, she could swear it was coming closer to her; but of course, that was not possible. Or was it? But the star was coming closer to Cupid, and the more she stared at it, the closer it came. Closer and closer came the star, until it was right outside her room. Cupid was so fixated on the star that she didn't see her parents standing in the doorway. They gave each other a quick, silent smile and then left to go to bed.

Cupid should've been nervous or scared, but for some reason, she just felt calm. The star inched its way inside her room. Suddenly, a soft low voice spoke to her. "I am Santa's Angel," said the voice. "Every year, on a reindeer's first birthday, if Santa has chosen that reindeer to get the gift of flight, he sends me to bestow it upon them."

Cupid was full of excitement. *Could this really be happening?* she thought.

Suddenly, a glittering shower came from the star and surrounded her. It was all tingly and warm. She could feel a certain energy growing within her.

She gazed up as the star began to look like a flame. The flame began to grow and grow, and she could hear someone calling her name: "Cupid! Cupid!" She looked up, and she wasn't in her room at all—she was sitting around a campfire with all the other reindeer.

Vixen leaned over to her and whispered in her ear, "Cupid, you've been daydreaming again, and you are muttering to yourself about Santa's Angel. You know you're not supposed to talk about that stuff in public."

"I know. I'm sorry. You know how I get sometimes," said Cupid. She was about to apologize to all the reindeer sitting around the campfire when there was a rustling in the trees behind them. All the reindeer jumped a little and looked back behind them.

Suddenly, Scooter burst out of the trees, nearly falling in the middle of the campfire. "Whoa!" he yelled. "How's everybody doing?"

After getting over their initial fright, the group of reindeer just shook their heads. Scooter went and sat down next to Comet. Comet liked Scooter, even though he seemed a little odd at times. His eyes were always bloodshot. He said it was because he had terrible allergies, but Comet wasn't quite sure if that was the truth.

"What were you doing in there?" she asked.

"Exploring," said Scooter.

"You shouldn't be out in the woods at night. There are bad things in there," said Comet.

Scooter gave Comet a long look. "It's fun. You should come with me sometime. How about tomorrow night?"

"I don't know," said Comet. "Isn't it kind of dangerous?"

Scooter was just about to answer her when he heard Mrs. White say, "Okay, children, time for bed."

All the reindeer got up from the campfire and started heading back toward the barracks.

"Meet me at the old well tomorrow night after sundown," said Scooter.

"Maybe," said Comet, and she smiled and gave him a little nudge.

The next night, as the sun was setting, Comet found herself standing next to the old well. She didn't know why she showed up, but there she was anyway, waiting for Scooter. It wasn't long before Scooter appeared.

"I didn't think you would make it," said Scooter.

Comet just looked at him and shrugged. "Well, where we going?"

Suddenly, they heard a creaking sound and Captain Jack appeared on the front porch of his office. "Quick, hide" whispered Scooter, and the ducked down behind the old well.

Captain Jack thought he had heard voices outside so he stepped out onto the porch to take a look. He could see vague outlines of the buildings and trees in the evening's moonlight.

Comet and Scooter were crouched behind the old well, nervously shaking. If they were caught they would be in big trouble. Just as they were at their peak of anxiety, Captain Jack turned and went back into his office. *Must have been the wind*, he thought.

Scooter gave Comet an anxious but sly look and said, "Let's go. We are going to meet some of my friends from the West Arctic." And off they went into the woods under the dark night sky.

The next morning, it was the day of the big soccer game against Moosehead Lodge. Donner was very excited, so he got up early. He knew his team was counting on him for a big day on the field. He decided to go to the cafeteria and see if there was any breakfast available that early in the morning. Of course, there was nobody there, but he grabbed some fruits and nuts and sat down to eat.

"Get up, you sleepyhead," said Vixen to Comet who seemed determined to sleep longer than the rest of the girls.

"**J**ust a little while longer," whined Comet, and she rolled over.

"Get up! It's the big game today, and we have to root for Dasher as she is going to play," said Vixen.

"Oh, all right," said Comet. She dropped her legs over the end of the bed, getting up groggily.

The crowd was buzzing as the game was about to begin. Everybody was there, including Mrs. White and the girls—Vixen, Cupid, and a not-so-awake Comet. Also in the crowd were their other friends Scarlet (the little red fox), Dottie (the frog with the golden crown), and Scooter (who arrived late as usual). Scarlet was still wearing the green scarf Vixen had given her after the Flight School test, since she had liked it so much.

Vixen leaned over to Dottie and asked her, "So why did you let those boys talk you into scaring us on that first night?"

"Because," Dottie said, "I like to a cause a little trouble sometimes, and there is a major upside to what I did."

"What's that?" asked Cupid.

"There is an old Klingon proverb—revenge is a dish best served cold. In other words, we can get them back for what they did. I've already talked to my friend Finchy about it, and he has agreed to help," said Dottie.

"I can get my friend Hedley to help us as well!" added Scarlet. At this, the girls leaned in close to each other and began to whisper their plans.

The game was just about to begin, and the boys and Dasher ran out to the field. The crowd cheered wildly. Donner, who took the center of the field, looked up at the moose approaching him. His eyes opened very wide as he saw what was looking down on him.

He had heard of this moose before; they called him ***The Masher***. He was a dark (almost black) color and had a large silver chain hanging from one of his antlers to his nose. His eyes were dark, and he is drooling slightly from his mouth.

Oh boy, thought Donner, but he was bound and determined to help his team as much as he could.

The referee dropped the ball to begin the game. Immediately, the moose started pushing the reindeer around, using their strength to gain an advantage. It wasn't long before ***The Masher*** had the ball. He ran down the field, knocking over several of the reindeer, and kicked the ball. Into the goal it went. Moosehead Lodge had scored the first goal.

Captain Jack immediately called a time-out and gathered the boys and Dasher together. "It's okay, don't get down on yourselves. Just remember what we practiced, and you'll be fine—play your game!" he barked out.

For the rest of the first half, the reindeer held their own. They used their speed and agility to dart around the moose. Just as halftime was beginning to approach, Dancer saw Donner make a quick break toward the Moosehead's goal. He kicked the ball as hard as he could, and it went right to Donner who kicked it into the net, and the reindeer had *scored a goal*! The game was tied 1–1! And the crowd are loving it! The whistle blew, and it was halftime. Both teams went to their sidelines to rest up before the second half began.

"Great job!" said Captain Jack to the team. "We can win this thing if you PLAY YOUR GAME!"

Donner, breathing heavily from all the running around he had been doing, turned to Dancer and said, "Thanks for the great pass, dude."

"No problem," Dancer replied, breathing heavily himself.

The second half of the game had begun, and it was much like the first. The reindeer were using their speed to zoom around the moose, but the moose were physically wearing them down. With just a few minutes left, Donner was chasing the ball down in the middle of the field. He didn't see **The Masher** bearing down on him. There was a huge collision, and both of them hit the ground.

There was a huge gasp from the crowd.

Prancer was sitting at the edge of the bench during the game, minding his own business, when he heard the loud groan. He stood up and looked out the field and saw that Donner was on the ground, not moving. **The Masher** was looking down at him. *This is not good*, he thought to himself.

Captain Jack and Mrs. White (who served as the team's nurse) were out on the field. After a while, Donner sat up. Captain Jack motioned to some of the boys to help carry Donner off the field. He looked dazed and a little bloody, but other than that, he was going to be all right.

Captain Jack turned to Prancer and said, "You're in." Prancer froze as his *worst* nightmare was about to come true. He absolutely, positively, did not want to get onto that field. But Captain Jack leaned over to him and—in a calm, reassuring voice—said, "Come on, son, do your best."

Prancer walked gingerly out on the field. He was just going to try and stay out of the way, and maybe he would be all right. There was just over a minute left in the game when Prancer looked down and saw that the ball was at his feet. He just about fainted. He looked up, and everyone was yelling at him: "Kick the ball! Kick the ball!"

He closed his eyes for just a second, and when he looked up, there was Dasher. He remembered that she told him if he got into any trouble, just kick the ball to her, and she would take care of him. So that's what he did. There were only a few seconds left in the game.

Dasher took the ball and zoomed around one moose; she zigzagged around

another, running down the field as fast as possible. She kicked the ball as hard as she could, and it went into the goal! Dasher had scored, and the reindeer had won the game!

The crowd ran onto the field and began congratulating Dasher, giving her high fives and slaps on the back, but Dasher went over to Prancer and just gave him a big hug. "You were terrific," she said. Prancer's face turned about as pink as his fur, but he was just happy it was all over. The other reindeer came over and were congratulating him as well.

Suddenly, Donner appeared, put his arm around Prancer, and said, "See, I told you he wasn't such a bad guy, after all."

The other reindeer nodded in agreement, and Mrs. White told Prancer, "If you want to be in dance class, that's fine with me." The other reindeer cheered, and Prancer just smiled and looked at the ground.

Captain Jack was beaming with pride as he walked into the middle of the team. "I am so proud of all of you." He leaned over to Donner with a concerned look on his face and said, "How are you?" And Donner just nodded that he was all right. He then turned to the boys and said, "Better keep practicing, boys, or she'll be better than all of you." And with that, he gave a great big smile.

They were about to leave the field to celebrate when Donner looked up, and standing right in front of him was the Masher. He leaned down and looked him right in the eyes and said "good game" and turned and walked off the field.

The victory celebration really didn't last that long because the next day was Family Day, where the relatives of the reindeer came and visited for lots of activities. Comet was particularly excited because she hadn't seen her little brother, Asteroid, for a while as he had been visiting relatives for the summer.

After breakfast, they all went down to Emuras Field, and all the moms, dads, brothers, and sisters of the reindeer were there. As soon as Asteroid saw Comet, he ran up to her and gave her a big hug. As they were milling around, she noticed Scooter was standing all by himself.

She went up to him and said, "Scooter, don't you have any family coming today?"

"No, my sister got sick, and they had to stay home," he said.

"That's too bad," said Comet. "You can join us." And she introduced him to her mom, dad, and her little brother, Asteroid.

The day was filled with games played in Emuras Field, swimming in Misty Lake, and lots of other activities. When it started to get dark, they built a big campfire and roasted marshmallows and talked about all the things that they had done during summer camp, including the great victory over the Moosehead Lodge.

Soon it was time for the young ones to go to bed, and Comet led Asteroid to the room where he was to sleep for the night. Just as she was leaving, Scooter turned to her and said, "Meet me at the old well in an hour."

"Okay, but not until Asteroid is asleep," she replied and gave him a slight grin.

Before they went to bed, Mrs. White read the younger children a short story. She tucked them in, turned out the lights, and went to join the other parents who had gathered in the cafeteria.

Comet met Scooter by the old well, and they disappeared into the forest as they had done several times in the last few days. However, this time, they didn't notice that they were being followed.

The Big Mean Wolf (whose parents had named him Drakh) was extremely angry. Not just regularly angry – but irritated and very, very grumpy. It had taken him a long time to recover from the wound inflicted by the reindeer's antlers (Captain Jack had saved Blitzen from being eaten by the Big Mean Wolf last spring by spearing him in the ribs).

He was going to make them pay, big time. He had noticed some other reindeer sneaking off into the forest late at night, and he was going to find out what they were doing and perhaps grab himself a little dinner.

He crouched down real low so he would not be noticed and began working his way through the forest trees.

Now we all know what little brothers like to do—they like to follow their big sisters around. Asteroid was no different. When he couldn't sleep, he looked out the window of his room and saw Scooter and Comet heading into the woods. He left his room and began to follow them.

When Drakh saw Asteroid, he thought to himself, *Now there is a tasty little morsel.* His stomach began to growl. He crawled very slowly as he began to circle his prey.

Comet stood straight up when she heard the scream coming from nearby in the woods. "What was that?" yelled Scooter.

"It sounded like my little brother, hurry!" said Comet, and she ran off into the woods.

Comet froze at the sight before her—the Big Mean Wolf had Asteroid pinned down on the ground with his arms. His mouth was open wide, showing very sharp teeth.

"STOP!" she cried and began running toward the Big Mean Wolf.

Drakh turned his head away from the already-battered Asteroid to face her. Just as Comet began to run toward Drakh, Scooter whisked past her and leaped into the air directly at the Big Mean Wolf. *This is all my fault*, he thought.

Drakh and Scooter collided midair with a loud crunching sound. The two began rolling around on the forest floor, arms and legs wildly hitting each other. Comet tried to help, but the last thing she remembered was the Big Mean Wolf's paw hitting her in the head and knocking her out as she fell to the ground.

The last thing Scooter thought, as the Big Mean Wolf's jaws dug into him, was *I'm sorry, Comet.*

Comet woke up a little disoriented. *Where am I?* she thought. When she realized she was in the hospital, the events from the previous night rushed back into her mind like a tidal wave. She opened her eyes, and standing directly above her were Captain Jack, Mrs. White, and—of all people—Santa.

"Where's Asteroid?" she managed to ask in a nervous and frightened voice.

"Calm down," said Captain Jack, and he patted her gently on the shoulder. "He's a little bruised, but he'll be okay. He's in a room down the hallway."

"And Scooter?"

Captain Jack shook his head from side to side. With a very sad look on his face, he said, "I'm sorry, he didn't make it. We found parts of him, but the wolf took the rest."

Comet began to cry, and Mrs. White put a gentle arm around her. "You've had a nasty bump on your head, my dear, but the doctor says you will be okay to go home tomorrow."

"What were you doing in the woods anyway?" she asked.

"Nothin'," said Comet, not wanting to tell them.

"Little lady, what were you doing in the woods?" said Captain Jack sternly.

She really, really did not want to tell them.

"I'll ask you one last time," said Captain Jack. "What were you and Scooter doing in the woods?"

Comet finally blurted it out, "Drugs, okay, it was drugs!"

Mrs. White let out a gasp, and her fur seemed to turn completely gray. Captain Jack snorted loudly and took a step back.

Santa looked at her for a very, very long time. His cheeks were super red. Finally, he spoke, "I'm very disappointed in you, young lady." Then he left the room with the other adults.

Comet closed her eyes and began to weep. "Never, never again," she said to herself. Her girlfriends—Cupid, Dasher, and Vixen—who had been waiting outside came into the room to comfort her. They didn't need to speak.

The next day, as Comet was getting ready to leave the hospital, Asteroid burst into the room and jumped into her arms. "I'm so, so sorry, little brother," she said and gave him a big hug.

Asteroid squeezed her back and said, "It's okay, Comet. I still love you."

"Please don't tell Mom and Dad," she begged him.

"They already know," said Mrs. White who had been standing in the doorway, and she entered the room. "They're in my office, waiting for you. I heard your mom and dad talking about a severe punishment."

"I don't care what it is," said Comet. "I deserve it."

Mrs. White leaned in very close to her and said, "What have you learned from this experience, young lady?"

Comet immediately said, "Sneaking around at night and doing things you're not supposed to be doing will turn out very, very bad."

"Well, when we leave here, you will be going home immediately!" said Mrs. White. And with that, the three of them left the room and headed back to summer camp.

A few days later, it was the end of summer camp, and the boys were in their barracks, packing up their belongings, getting ready to go home, and discussing recent events.

"I can't believe that's what they were doing," said Dancer. "One of us should've punched them in the head."

"That's not very nice and probably wouldn't have done much good anyway," said Blitzen.

"I hear Comet is grounded, like, forever," said Prancer.

"At least until Flight School starts in a few weeks. I hear Santa is going to let her attend despite what happened, although she will be on probation for the first semester," said Donner.

The boys were continuing their discussion when Prancer suddenly looked up. "Guys," he said. "Um, guys!" The other boys still weren't paying any attention to him, so he reached down and tilted Donner's head upward. "Look," he whispered.

Crouched in the doorway was a giant alligator looking right at them. The alligator took a couple of steps forward and opened its huge jaws, showing them several rows of very sharp teeth.

The boys quickly stood up back-to-back.

"Geschmergal!" exclaimed Blitzen.

"What does that mean?" asked Prancer.

"It means *holy crap*" replied Blitzen.

"So what should we do?" asked Dancer.

"**Q**uick, out the back door," said Donner, and they began to run toward the back of the barracks. They stopped in their tracks when standing in the back doorway was a huge brown bear. The enormous bear stood up on its hind legs, spread its claws wide, and let out a loud growl.

"Now what?" asked Dancer.

Donner looked at his friends. "I don't know. Back the other way, I guess."

They ran toward the front door, but the alligator was still there. The boys were huddled together with no way out. Sweat began to run down their faces. They were trapped!

Suddenly, they heard a faint giggle outside the window. Then another and another. They looked again toward the front door, and standing there was Dottie. "I see you met my friend Finchy!" she said with a smile on her face.

The giant alligator sat up on his hind legs, smiled, and waved at the boys.

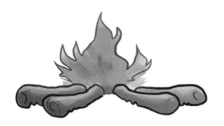

"**A**nd my friend Hedley!" they heard from behind them.

They turned around to see Scarlet standing in the doorway next to the giant bear. The bear sat down, threw a plaid scarf around his neck, and began picking his teeth with his claw.

The girls could hardly contain themselves as they ran into the boys' barracks, giggling and laughing.

"That's not funny," said all the boys at once.

"Oh, yes it is. Yes it is," all the girls agreed.

And as they left summer camp and headed toward home, you could hear a faint "Ho, Ho, Ho!" in the distance. It echoed throughout the Arctic for some time.

The End

Afterword

To my Adult Readers:

Please be aware that I did my due diligence before putting anything like drugs into *Summer Camp*. I interviewed numerous parents with children of all ages and asked them this question, "If you had a vehicle to discuss what I call *teenage issues* with your child at an early age, would you welcome it?" To a letter, they all emphatically said yes.

Many of them expressed how difficult it was for them to discuss these kinds of issues with their children, even those in their teenage years. I think you would agree that with the abundance of media now available, children are exposed to all kinds of social issues and behaviors at earlier ages than ever before.

Think of this as a way for you to open up uncomfortable dialogue with your children that could potentially instill trust between you for many years to come. After all, they're not stupid. And if you don't talk to them about these things, most likely, their friends will—and that will more than likely lead to misinformation and bad choices.

Take care.

As a longtime marketing researcher, Michael McWade has devoted his life to determining how both adults and children make choices. He has studied their motivations, passions, and desires toward the goal of a fulfilled and happy life. McWade's books are designed not just to entertain but expose children to valuable life lessons early to guide them in making apt life-related choices.

Mike has always had an ingenious quality when telling a story – especially capturing the interest of children. He is the only adult who is begged to sit at the kid's table during a party.

www.michaelmcwade.com

Facebook.com/TheReindeerChronicles

Printed in the United States
By Bookmasters